OUR CLASS MEMORY Album

by Kimberly Colen
and Nanci Lane

SCHOLASTIC
PROFESSIONAL BOOKS

NEW YORK • TORONTO • LONDON • AUCKLAND • SYDNEY

To all who make a difference in the future of our children.

Special thanks to Cynthia Maloney for her encouragement.
K.C. & N.L.

Text and interior design by Antler and Baldwin, Inc.
Cover design by Vincent Ceci
Cover and page illustrations by Jan Pyk

ISBN 0-590-49416-3
Copyright © 1993 by Kimberly Colen and Nanci Lane. All rights reserved.
12 11 10 9 8 7 6 5 4 3 2   7 8 9 0 / 9
Printed in the U.S.A.

TABLE OF CONTENTS

INTRODUCTION

OUR CLASS MEMORY ALBUM is a journal, a photo album, an annual, a record keeper, and an organizer all in one. You can use this book for any grade or subject you teach to serve as a keepsake of the highlights of one year, a reminder of the people and events that made the year unique. You and your students will want to look at this book over and over again, year after year.

OUR CLASS MEMORY ALBUM is a place to record observations and discoveries throughout the year. Invite your students and the people who assist you during the school year to help fill in the pages. Their participation will give the book a special dimension you'll treasure in years to come.

OUR CLASS MEMORY ALBUM consists of fill-in pages on which to record everything from fall festivities to current trends, from field trips outside the classroom to guests invited inside. There's room for a photo of each student and for one of the entire class. You'll find pages for hobbies, favorite authors, and memorable quotes. There's even a page for the classroom pet! You'll find space for students' special notes and artwork and pages where your former students can greet new students. At the end, there's room for year-end autographs and good-byes, and of course there's much more in between.

We hope you'll keep this book in your classroom to use at any time during any week, month, or season. Have a wonderful year, and may it be one filled with a lifetime of memories.

USING THIS BOOK

This book is easy to use. There is only a right way—and that is *your* way. Based on your classroom experiences this year, the unique book you and your students create will be filled with your mementos.

This section offers suggestions on effective ways to put this book to use. You'll find ideas on how you can use this album with your students, their guardians, your coworkers, and classroom guests.

What can you do if you find a page that's inapplicable to you or your classroom? Simply duplicate a page you'd like an extra copy of and glue it on top of the page you won't need. Be sure to copy the original page before filling it in.

You may want to have students start filling in some pages early in the year. Reading about each other's hobbies and interests, jobs, or favorite authors is one way students can get to know their classmates.

Keep this book in the class library for students to look at and enjoy throughout the year. You may also find that students will use the class memory book as a model for their own albums.

Enjoy and have fun!

Our Class Memory Album (cover)—Start by personalizing your book. Fill in the school year in the blanks provided on the cover.

Welcome from Last Year's Class (page 8)—Ask students from last year's class to fill in their comments about what they liked about being in your class and what they'll miss. Give them a chance to offer advice to incoming students. Ask for comments on favorite units, activities, or projects. For children too young to write, ask them to dictate their thoughts and comments so that you can jot them down for your new students.

At the end of the year, have your present class begin next year's book by filling in these pages while their thoughts are still fresh.

Our Class Picture (page 10)—Attach your class picture at the front of the book to help remind you of who's who in future years.

Special Notes from Students (page 18)—When a student gives you a letter with a personal message, a note with a few beginning words, or a proud first-time signature, you can save those keepsakes here.

Views of the News (page 22)—Allow older students to use these pages as a forum for their views and opinions of what's happening in the world. Let them express their thoughts verbally in an open and secure classroom setting and then in writing. For younger children, discuss something in the news that you feel directly affects them. Write down their opinions, comments, and concerns.

Ideas & Innovations (page 24)—Use these pages as a grab bag for ideas and contributions from your students, their parents, or your coworkers that helped make life in the classroom run smoothly and efficiently. Jot down organizational ideas, new methods for taking attendance, homework or test-taking strategies, and ways to promote values and ethics in the classroom.

The Most Important Events of the Year (page 26)—From the smallest detail to a significant milestone, these are things you want to remember about the year. You may want to include special assemblies, book or science fairs, and school-wide events like field days.

Great Walls & Bulletin Boards (page 31)—Photographs are your best reminders when you want to recreate a wall decoration or prepare a successful unit bulletin board again.

Kids at Work (page 32)—Let students who have outside jobs fill in the information here. If your students are too young to have a formal job or have household chores, instead allow them to describe and write about what they are responsible for at home.

We Get Excited About... (page 36)—Ask students to add to this page when they show special interest or excitement about a particular theme or unit. Their comments will provide you with a comprehensive running list of your students' favorite topics.

Artists at Work (page 37)—Here's room for designs, greeting cards, and drawings. You may also want to add photos of larger pieces of artwork students take home.

Our Hobbies & Interests (page 40)—Make sure you participate by filling in your name and hobbies too!

School News (page 50)—Record the most memorable events that took place in and around your school. If possible, get quotes from the people involved. Include photographs, captions, and headlines. If your students are too young to fill in these pages, allow them to provide quotes or draw pictures about school events.

Here We Are (page 52)—Ask each student for a school picture to attach here, and have children sign their names.

Souvenir Page (page 62)—This is a good place to attach anything you want to save and can't quite find another spot for. Or attach your duplicate pages here. For example, if you went on three more field trips that you've recorded on duplicate pages, tape or glue them to these pages. If you like, create your own fill-in pages here to record your unique memories of this year.

*Memory is the diary that
we all carry about with us.*
—OSCAR WILDE

This book is dedicated to
_____
_____
_____

This book belongs to_____
Grade_____ Section_____
School_____
Address_____ Phone_____
Principal_____
19_____

WELCOME FROM

Great is the art of beginning,
but greater the art is of ending.
—Longfellow

Read welcome notes, comments, and advice from last year's class.

LAST YEAR'S CLASS

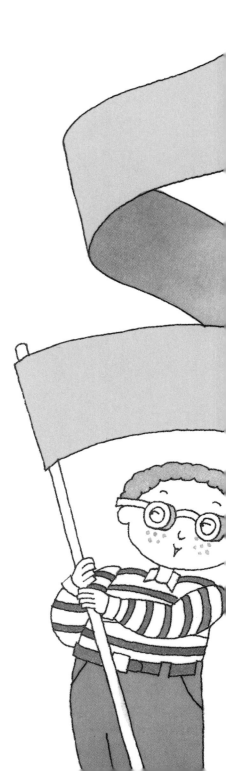

OUR CLASS PICTURE

OUR CLASS

*How casually and unobservedly
we make all our most valued acquaintances.*
—EMERSON

Student's Names

_____   _____

_____   _____

_____   _____

_____   _____

_____   _____

_____   _____

_____   _____

_____   _____

_____   _____

_____   _____

_____   _____

FALL
ACTIVITIES & FESTIVITIES

Fall means back to school, new friends, falling leaves, jack-o'-lanterns, and time for giving thanks. Fall also brings holidays and special days. Here are some of the things we did and ways we celebrated.

Event:_____

Date:_____

What we did:_____

Event:_____

Date:_____

What we did:_____

Event:_____

Date:_____

What we did:_____

_____

_____

_____

_____

_____

_____

_____

_____

Event:_____

Date:_____

What we did:_____

_____

_____

_____

_____

_____

_____

_____

_____

WINTER
ACTIVITIES & FESTIVITIES

Winter means cold weather, end-of-year holiday celebrations, remembering important people, and hearts and ground hogs. Here are some of the things we did and ways we celebrated.

Event:_____

Date:_____

What we did:_____

_____

_____

_____

_____

_____

_____

_____

_____

_____

Event:_____

Date:_____

What we did:_____

_____

_____

_____

_____

_____

_____

_____

_____

_____

_____

_____

_____

Event:_____

Date:_____

What we did:_____

_____

_____

_____

_____

_____

_____

_____

_____

_____

Event:_____

Date:_____

What we did:_____

_____

_____

_____

_____

_____

_____

_____

_____

_____

_____

SPRING
ACTIVITIES & FESTIVITIES

Springtime means shamrocks, longer days, carnivals, field days, chicks and bunnies, and greenery all around us. Here are some of the things we did and ways we celebrated.

Event:_____

Date:_____

What we did:_____

_____

_____

_____

_____

_____

_____

_____

_____

_____

_____

Event:_____

Date:_____

What we did:_____

_____

_____

_____

_____

_____

_____

_____

_____

_____

_____

_____

Event:_____

Date:_____

What we did:_____

_____

_____

_____

_____

_____

_____

_____

_____

_____

_____

Event:_____

Date:_____

What we did:_____

_____

_____

_____

_____

_____

_____

_____

_____

_____

_____

_____

Special Notes FROM STUDENTS

Mementos to save and cherish.

OUR CLASS FAVORITES

Every generation laughs at the old fashions,
but follows religiously the new.
—THOREAU

Favorite Popular Songs

Favorite Movie Stars

Favorite Movies

Trendiest Fashions

Favorite TV Shows

Favorite TV Stars

Favorite Amusement

Favorite Food Craze

Favorite Phrases or Expressions

VIEWS OF THE NEWS

These events made headlines locally, nationally, or internationally, and we have opinions to express.

Attach headline here:

Our opinions:_____

_____

_____

Attach headline here:

Our opinions:_____

_____

_____

Attach newspaper or magazine articles and photographs here.

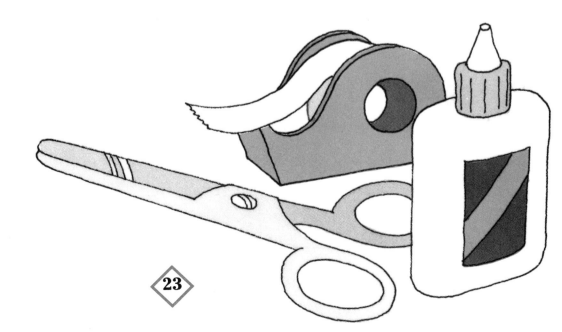

IDEAS & INNOVATIONS

To have ideas is to gather flowers;
to think is to weave them into garlands.
—MADAME SWETCHINE

Here are some of the creative ideas and tips that worked particularly well in our classroom this year.

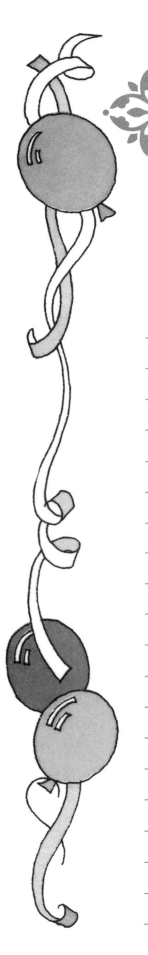

THE MOST IMPORTANT EVENTS OF THE YEAR

Here are the events that were too important to forget.

FIELD TRIPS

*Experience, travel—these
are an education in themselves.*
—EURIPIDES

Place:_____

Date:_____

All about our trip:_____

_____

_____

_____

_____

_____

Favorite things on our trip:_____

_____

_____

_____

_____

_____

_____

Would we go again?_____

Place:_____

Date:_____

All about our trip:_____

_____

_____

_____

_____

_____

Favorite things on our trip:_____

_____

_____

_____

_____

_____

Would we go again?_____

Place:_____

Date:_____

All about our trip:_____

_____

_____

_____

_____

Favorite things on our trip:_____

_____

_____

_____

_____

_____

Would we go again?_____

Place:_____

Date:_____

All about our trip:_____

_____

_____

_____

_____

Favorite things on our trip:_____

_____

_____

_____

_____

_____

Would we go again?_____

SCHOOL & COMMUNITY PROJECTS

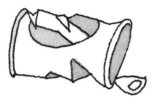

*Our deeds determine us,
as much as we determine our deeds.*
—GEORGE ELIOT

These are ways we tried to make the world a better place.

Project:_____

_____

_____

_____

_____

_____

Purpose of the project:_____

_____

_____

_____

_____

_____

What we did:_____

_____

_____

_____

_____

_____

Project:_____

_____

_____

_____

_____

_____

Purpose of the project:_____

_____

_____

_____

_____

_____

What we did:_____

_____

_____

_____

_____

_____

GREAT WALLS & BULLETIN BOARDS

These are our favorite classroom wall decorations.

KIDS AT WORK

I'm a great believer in luck, and I find
the harder I work the more I have of it.
—THOMAS JEFFERSON

These are some of the jobs we did outside the classroom.

Name:_____

My job:_____

_____

_____

What I like about my job:_____

_____

_____

Name:_____

My job:_____

_____

_____

What I like about my job:_____

_____

_____

Attach announcements, clippings, and photos here.

Name:_____

My job:_____

_____

_____

What I like about my job:_____

_____

_____

Name:_____

My job:_____

_____

_____

What I like about my job:_____

_____

_____

Name:_____

My job:_____

_____

_____

What I like about my job:_____

_____

_____

Attach announcements, clippings, and photos here.

Name:_____

My job:_____

_____

_____

What I like about my job:_____

_____

_____

Name:_____

My job:_____

_____

_____

What I like about my job:_____

_____

_____

Attach announcements, clippings, and photos here.

COMPUTERS

Computers provided us with new ideas, new problem-solving techniques, and new communication methods. These are ways we used them.

How we used the computer in our classroom:_____

_____

_____

Things we can do now that we couldn't do before:_____

_____

_____

Using computers individually, students like to:_____

_____

Using computers on group projects, students enjoy:_____

_____

WE GET EXCITED ABOUT ...

Favorite things we learned in our class.

Artists at Work

Here are some of our artistic creations.

OUR HOBBIES & INTERESTS

Here is what we liked doing when we were not in school.

Name	Hobby/Hobbies

Name	Hobby/Hobbies

CLASSROOM BOOKSHELF

A good book is the best of friends,
the same today and forever.
—MARTIN TUPPER

Written on the book spines are the titles and authors of the books we enjoyed most.

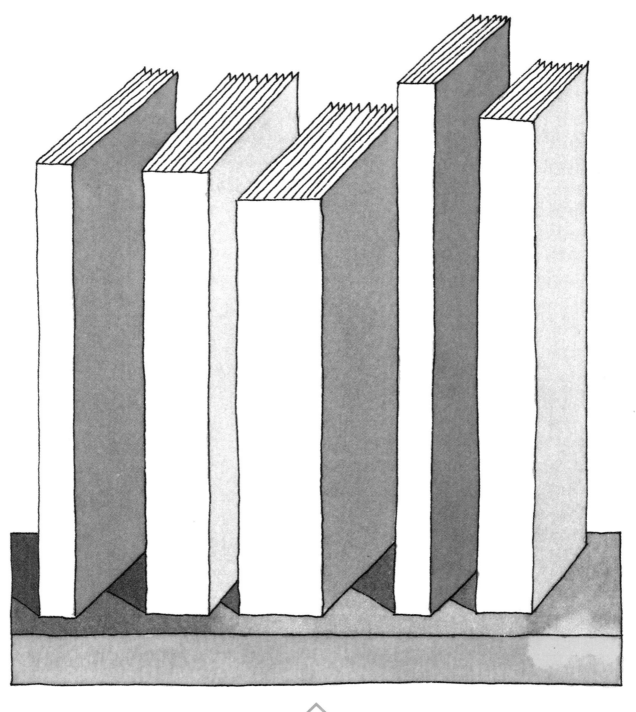

OUR FAVORITE
AUTHORS & ILLUSTRATORS

Here are some of our favorite authors and illustrators.

SHOW

These are some of the shows we put on.

Date:_____

Show:_____

What we did:
(skit, play, puppet show, etc.)_____

_____

Photos:

TIME

Date:_____

Show:_____

What we did:
(skit, play, puppet show, etc.)_____

_____

Photos:

"QUOTABLE

I'll always remember these remarks and comments from my students.

We were discussing_____

when_____ said:

"_____

_____"

We were discussing_____

when_____ said:

"_____

_____"

We were discussing_____

when_____ said:

"_____

_____"

QUOTES "

We were discussing _____

when _____ said:

" _____

_____ "

We were discussing _____

when _____ said:

" _____

_____ "

We were discussing _____

when _____ said:

" _____

_____ "

WELCOMED GUESTS

*Good company and good discourse are
the very sinews of virtue.*
—Izaak Walton

These guests visited our classroom.

Name:_____

Occupation:_____

Reason for visit:_____

Guest's signature and comment:_____

_____

_____

_____

_____

_____

_____

Name:_____

Occupation:_____

Reason for visit:_____

Guest's signature and comment:_____

_____

_____

_____

_____

_____

_____

Name:_____

Occupation:_____

Reason for visit:_____

Guest's signature and comment:_____

_____

_____

_____

_____

_____

Name:_____

Occupation:_____

Reason for visit:_____

Guest's signature and comment:_____

_____

_____

_____

_____

_____

Name:_____

Occupation:_____

Reason for visit:_____

Guest's signature and comment:_____

_____

_____

_____

_____

_____

Name:_____

Occupation:_____

Reason for visit:_____

Guest's signature and comment:_____

_____

_____

_____

_____

_____

SCHOOL NEWS

These are the things that made news at our school.

# HERE WE ARE

Name

Name

Name

Name

Name

Name

Name

Name

Name

Name

Name

Name

Name

Name

Name

Name

Name

Name

Name

Name

Name

Name

Name

Name

Name

Name

Name

Name

Name

Name

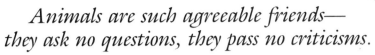

PET CORNER

Animals are such agreeable friends—
they ask no questions, they pass no criticisms.
—GEORGE ELLIOT

These pets shared our classroom.

Type of pet:_____

Name:_____

What our pet eats:_____

Our pet's special characteristics:_____

_____

Date:_____

Our pet stayed at the home of:

_____

_____

_____

_____

Name:_____

Type of pet:_____

What our pet eats:_____

Our pet's special characteristics:_____

_____

Our pet stayed at the home of:

Date:_____

_____

_____

_____

_____

CANDIDS

How beautiful is youth! How bright it gleams
With its illusions, aspirations, dreams!
—LONGFELLOW

Here are pictures that remind us of the good times we had.

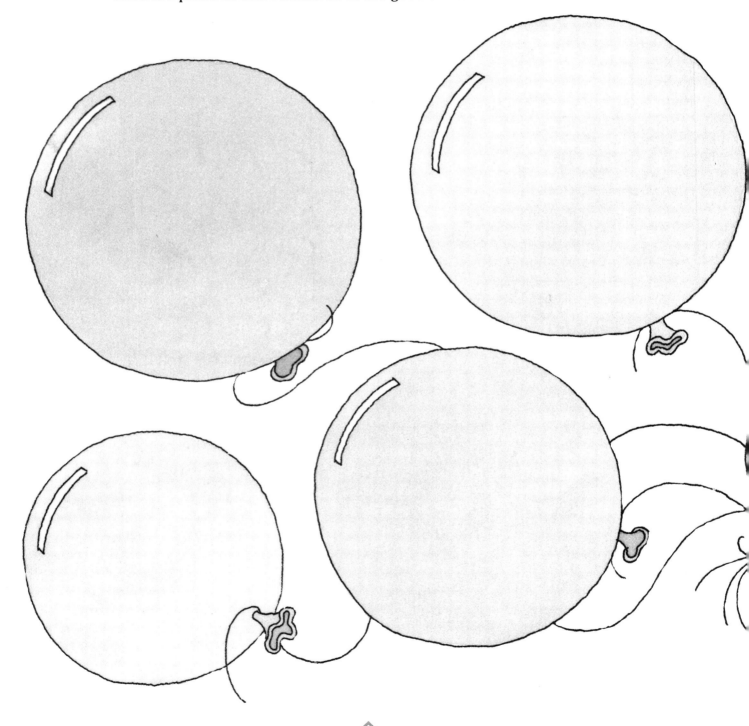

Our Autographs

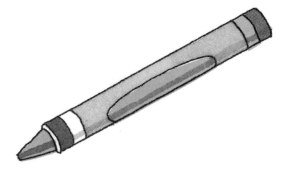

SOUVENIR PAGES